MAR - - 2021

Help Me Understand

What Do I Do When People I Know Are Racist?

Caitie McAneney

PowerKiDS
press™

NEW YORK

Published in 2020 by The Rosen Publishing Group, Inc.
29 East 21st Street, New York, NY 10010

First Edition

Editor: Rachel Gintner
Book Design: Rachel Rising

Photo Credits: Cover LightField Studios/Shuttterstock.com; p. 5 Atomazul/Shutterstock.com; p. 7 GagliardiPhotography/Shutterstock.com; p. 8 Phovoir/Shutterstock.com; p. 9 TheVisualsYouNeed/Shutterstock.com; p. 10 MAHATHIR MOHD YASIN/Shutterstock.com; pp. 11, 12 Africa Studio/Shutterstock.com; p. 13 Iakov Filimonov/Shutterstock.com; p. 14 Catalin Petolea/Shutterstock.com; p. 15 Olimpik/Shutterstock.com; p. 17 Rawpixel.com/Shutterstock.com; p. 18 Blaj Gabriel/Shutterstock.com; p. 19 Photographee.eu/Shutterstock.com; p. 21 Sergey Novikov/Shutterstock.com; p. 22 pixelheadphoto digitalskillet/Shutterstock.com.

Cataloging-in-Publication Data

Names: McAneney, Caitie.
Title: What do I do when people I know are racist? / Caitie McAneney.
Description: New York : PowerKids Press, 2020. | Series: Help me understand | Includes glossary and index.
Identifiers: ISBN 9781725309463 (pbk.) | ISBN 9781725309487 (library bound) | ISBN 9781725309470 (6 pack)
Subjects: LCSH: Racism–Juvenile literature. | Prejudices–Juvenile literature.
Classification: LCC HT1521.M39 2020 | DDC 305.8–dc23

Manufactured in the United States of America

CPSIA Compliance Information: Batch #CWPK20. For Further Information contact Rosen Publishing, New York, New York at 1-800-237-9932.

Some of the images in this book illustrate individuals who are models. The depictions do not imply actual situations or events.

Contents

What Are Racism and Prejudice?

Everyone's different. We wear different clothes, speak different languages, have different skin colors, and believe different things. This is called diversity. We can support diversity by being fair and open to those who are different from us.

However, some people don't accept differences. They think they're better than others of a different race. This is called racism. Some judge others based on their skin color, **religion**, or where they come from. This is prejudice. Prejudice and racism are very hurtful.

Racism has been a problem for a long time. In 1963, Dr. Martin Luther King Jr. said he dreamed that his children would be judged "not by the color of their skin but by the content of their character."

Understanding Privilege

It's upsetting to learn that someone you know is racist. There may be many reasons why this is the case. One reason is **privilege**. Some people don't recognize that their skin color makes them privileged. For example, white, wealthy people have often taken and been given privilege in our society.

Groups of people have had privilege around the world and throughout history. People from privileged groups are more likely to land jobs, make more money at those jobs, and move ahead in society. That can make it hard for people from **minority** groups to get ahead.

Prejudice keeps privilege in business. Imagine you get extra credit for answering questions in class. But your teacher only calls on white students. How can other students get that extra credit?

Racism Hurts

Racism is very hurtful. It creates a separation between people who could otherwise be friends. It takes opportunities away from people who are **qualified**. It attacks people who have done nothing wrong.

If you're from a minority group, you probably know the power of racism all too well. Some people might look at you differently. People might not listen to what you have to say. People might say hurtful things or call you hurtful names. No one wins when racism is in the mix.

If you're from a minority group, you may have been on the receiving end of racist comments. Remember that such remarks aren't fair, and that you should be treated with respect.

9

Racist Remarks

Throughout history, people have been treated unfairly because of their race. Some have been passed over for teams, schools, and jobs. Some people have been beaten or even killed. These are **extreme** racist actions. Everyday racism often includes racist remarks or small actions.

Have you ever heard someone say something racist? It might be as simple as a white student saying "I wouldn't want *her* on my team" about a student of color. Or, it might be someone saying someone else is dumb, lazy, or sneaky based on their race.

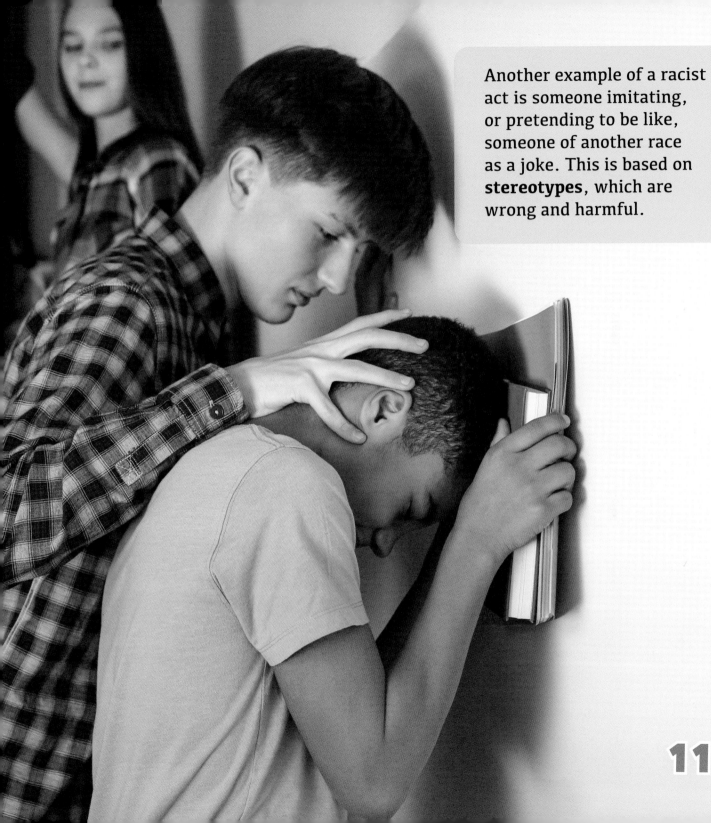

Another example of a racist act is someone imitating, or pretending to be like, someone of another race as a joke. This is based on **stereotypes**, which are wrong and harmful.

11

Racist Relatives

Being attacked by racism is painful. But what if you aren't the one being attacked? What if you know and love the person who's being racist? That can be painful too.

Imagine you're at a fun family dinner, talking to loved ones. But then your favorite uncle says that all people of a certain race are **violent**. You have friends of that race. You know they aren't violent. You don't know what to do or say. What can you do?

Dealing with racist relatives or friends is hard. You can use special tools to deal with these hard **situations**.

13

Disagreeing with Respect

You've probably learned to always treat your relatives with respect. That makes a situation involving racism extra hard. How can you disagree with them but also show respect?

First, try to take the other person's perspective, or point of view. Why might they think that way? They may have learned this way of thinking from other family or friends. If you say something, keep your voice calm. Tell your opinion and be truthful. Don't yell at that person—even if it's hard not to.

An example of disagreeing respectfully would be, "Excuse me, but my best friend is that race. She is a wonderful person, and it hurts me to hear you say those things."

15

Showing Empathy for Others

You can also deal with racist loved ones by showing in addition to telling. Show them how to have empathy for people who are different from them. Empathy means understanding and sharing how another person is feeling.

One way to show empathy is to listen to others. If your friend is being treated unfairly based on race, listen to their story. Learn from it. Make friends with people from different races and backgrounds. Do things in your community and meet new kinds of people.

If your racist friend or family member sees that you're friends with someone of another race, they might realize that it's not fair to treat others with prejudice.

Educating Others

What if you know your loved one isn't usually a bad person, but they're still being unfairly racist? They might not have the knowledge that you have about empathy and fairness. In this case, you can teach them what you know.

Tell your loved one about how harmful prejudice is. You might say, "It's very harmful to others when they're not judged by their true character. How would you feel if you were treated that way?" Talk to them about privilege and harmful stereotypes.

Some people aren't called on to think of their prejudice in a new light. They don't know how harmful they're being. You can teach them what you know.

19

Overcoming Stereotypes

Imagine you wore blue one day. Then someone said, "Anyone who wears blue is dumb!" You were being treated unfairly because of a stereotype made up by your classmate. Now, imagine that happened every day for something you couldn't control—your race.

Stereotypes start in communities and **cultures** when people don't get to know people who are different from them as individuals. Stereotypes are widespread and harmful. You can overcome stereotypes by remembering and reminding others that all people are individuals.

One way to get past stereotypes is to meet people of different races and backgrounds. You will soon see—and be able to tell others—how wrong stereotypes really are.

Stand Up for What's Right!

When someone you know is racist, you might feel helpless. Maybe you're on the receiving end of the racist remark or action. Maybe you're just an observer. Either way, you can stand up for what's right.

Taking a stand isn't easy, especially against someone you know and love. However, if you speak calmly, show empathy, and state your facts, you'll do your part. You might even change their mind. And *that* is how we make the world a better place!

Glossary

culture: The beliefs and ways of life of a certain group of people.

extreme: Very great in degree.

minority: Having to do with a group of people who are different from the larger group in a country or other area in some way, such as race or religion.

privilege: A right or advantage given to a certain person or group.

qualified: Capable and educated in a certain subject or role; able to do something.

religion: The belief in a god or a group of gods.

situation: All the facts, conditions, and events that affect someone or something in a certain time and place.

stereotype: An unfair and untrue belief that many people have about all people or things in a particular group.

violent: Involving the use of force to cause harm.

Index

Websites

Due to the changing nature of Internet links, PowerKids Press has developed an online list of websites related to the subject of this book. This site is updated regularly. Please use this link to access the list: www.powerkidslinks.com/HMU/racist